This Topsy and Tim
book belongs to

_____

Topsy + Tim

make a new friend

Jean and Gareth Adamson

Ladybird

This story was inspired by Lisa Gardner
and the Fawcett Primary School, Cambridge.
It is dedicated to the memory of Lisa.

All Ladybird books are available at most bookshops, supermarkets
and newsagents, or can be ordered direct from:
Ladybird Postal Sales PO Box 133 Paignton TQ3 2YP England
Telephone: (+44) 01803 554761 *Fax:* (+44) 01803 663394

A catalogue record for this book is available from the British Library

Published by Ladybird Books Ltd
A subsidiary of the Penguin Group
A Pearson Company

© Jean and Gareth Adamson MCMXCV
This edition MCMXCVIII

The moral rights of the author/illustrator have been asserted

LADYBIRD and the device of a Ladybird are trademarks of Ladybird Books Ltd Loughborough Leicestershire UK

Topsy and Tim were playing in the park
when they met a little girl in a wheelchair.
'Hello,' said Topsy. 'What's your name?'
'I'm Jenny,' said the little girl, shyly.
'We're Topsy and Tim and we're twins,'
said Topsy.

'I like your wheelchair, Jenny,' said Tim.
'What makes it go?'
'Guess,' said Jenny.
'Mmmm – a battery?' guessed Tim.
Jenny laughed. 'No,' she said.
'I turn the wheels with my hands.
I'm very strong.'

Jenny whizzed her wheelchair along
and Topsy and Tim raced after her.
Their mums sat on a bench and watched.
'Careful, Topsy and Tim!' called Mummy.
When it was time to go home, Topsy and Tim
waved goodbye to their new friend.
'See you again soon, Jenny,' called Topsy.

When Topsy and Tim arrived at school on Monday morning, Miss Terry said, 'A new girl is coming to join us today. Her name is Jenny and she uses a wheelchair.'
Topsy and Tim guessed that Jenny might be their friend from the park.

'Why does Jenny use a wheelchair?'
asked Vinda.
'Because her legs don't work properly,'
said Miss Terry. 'When a part of
someone's body or brain doesn't work
properly we say they have a disability.'

'Can anyone think of more disabilities?'
asked Miss Terry.
'My uncle's deaf, so he wears a hearing
aid to help him hear,' said Tony Welch.
'My eyes need glasses to help me see
properly,' said Stevie Dunton.

'Some grown-ups who can't see have a guide dog to help them,' said Topsy. Andy Anderson shut his eyes and tried to walk across the room, but he soon bumped into a table.

Everyone laughed at Andy, except
Miss Terry.
'It's very unkind to laugh at, or to
tease, someone who is different,' said
Miss Terry. 'I hope you children will
never, NEVER do such an unkind thing.'

'We won't,' promised all the children.

When Jenny arrived with her classroom
helper, all the children came to say hello.
Jenny was feeling shy, so she was glad
to see Topsy and Tim's friendly faces.
Miss Terry asked the twins to look after
Jenny as she was new.

Topsy and Tim showed Jenny round
the classroom.
'We keep our things in these drawers,'
said Tim. 'This one is mine.'
One of the drawers had a new label.
It said 'Jenny'.
'Here's my drawer,' said Jenny.

Topsy and Tim took Harriet Hamster
out of her cage to show Jenny.
'Would you like to weigh her?' asked Topsy.
Jenny put Harriet on the scales. 'She weighs
one hundred grammes,' said Tim.

The bell rang and it was time for break.
Kerry held the door wide open for Jenny
and her wheelchair. Topsy and Tim
showed the way to the ramp that led to
the playground. Jenny whizzed down the
ramp in her wheelchair.

After break, Miss Terry said, 'Harriet
Hamster has escaped from her cage.
Someone left the cage door open.'
'It was Topsy and me,' said Tim sadly.
'We were showing Harriet to Jenny.'
'Everyon   lease keep a lookout for
Harriet,'   id Miss Terry.

It was time to do some number work.
'I've forgotten what four looks like,'
said Topsy.
Jenny wrote a figure 4.
'I remember,' said Topsy.
Jenny was good at numbers.

At lunchtime, all the children
had to go and wash their hands.
'I've got my own special toilet, with
a washbasin,' said Jenny.
She showed it to Topsy and Tim.
'It's big enough for Jenny's wheelchair
too,' explained Sue, the helper.

Afternoon lessons began with PE
and Jenny joined in everything.
She whirled around the hall in her
wheelchair.
'Ouch!' said Andy Anderson. 'Jenny's
wheelchair trod on my toe!'

The afternoon ended quietly, with
Miss Terry reading a story to the children.
They all sat on the carpet, listening – and
Jenny sat on the carpet, too.

Mr Taylor, the head teacher, came into the
classroom to see how Jenny was getting on.
He was surprised to see her empty wheelchair.
'Where is Jenny?' he asked.
'She's here with us,' said Tim, waving
to Mr Taylor.

'Jenny got out of her wheelchair
all by herself,' said Topsy.
'I can get back into my wheelchair
all by myself, too,' said Jenny.
Everyone watched while Jenny wriggled
across the floor and pulled herself up
into her chair. It was hard work and it
took a long time, but in the end she
did it.

'Well done, Jenny!' said Mr Taylor,
and everybody clapped. They all felt
very proud of Jenny.

At hometime, Jenny's mother came into
the classroom. She found Jenny with
a big smile on her face.
'Hello, Mum,' she said. 'This is my drawer
and look what I've found in it.'
Jenny opened her drawer – and up popped
Harriet Hamster.
'Hooray!' shouted Topsy and Tim. 'Jenny's
found Harriet Hamster.'